BTLC

Titles in Horror Hotel:

NIGHTMARE MAN
TIM COLLINS & ABBY RYDER

WALL CRAWLERS
TIM COLLINS & JAMES LAWRENCE

BED BUGS
TIM COLLINS & JAMES LAWRENCE

THE MIRROR
TIM COLLINS & JAMES LAWRENCE

THE LIFT
TIM COLLINS & ABBY RYDER

THIEF
TIM COLLINS & ABBY RYDER

Badger Publishing Limited, Oldmedow Road,
Hardwick Industrial Estate, King's Lynn PE30 4JJ

Telephone: 01438 791037
www.badgerlearning.co.uk

Wall Crawlers 978-1-78837-418-7

2 4 6 8 10 9 7 5 3 1

Illustration: James Lawrence

Tim Collins

Illustrated by James Lawrence

Contents

Chapter 1	The Noise	6
Chapter 2	Secret Room	12
Chapter 3	Trapped	20
Questions		31
Meet the Author and Illustrator		32

Story Vocabulary
scratching
noise
screwed

The story so far...

Nadia and Amy were on their way to visit friends, but Nadia's bike got a puncture and it was raining.

They saw an old hotel.

"We'll have to stay here for the night," said Amy.

"Welcome to Horror Hotel," said a woman. "I am the Manager. I hope you enjoy your stay with us."

They didn't really want to stay in this strange hotel, but they knew it would only be for one night.

What could possibly go wrong? they thought.

Chapter 1
The Noise

Nadia couldn't sleep.

There was a scratching noise coming from the room next door.

It was like someone was running their nails down the wall.

Nadia couldn't stand the scratching noise any more.

She had to find out what it was.

Amy was in the room next door.

Nadia knocked on her door.

"Please stop scratching on the wall," said Nadia. "I can't sleep."

"But I wasn't scratching on the wall,"
said Amy. "I thought it was you."

Then Nadia felt scared.

The noise must have been coming from
inside the wall.

Chapter 2

Secret Room

The girls saw a piece of wood screwed to the wall.

Amy pulled away the piece of wood.

Behind it was a dark hole.

A horrible smell was coming from it.

The scratching noise got louder.

Something was coming towards them.

"I don't like this," said Nadia. "I'm going to get the Manager. There might be rats."

Amy tried to put the piece of wood back, but something pushed it from the other side.

Nadia screamed.

A slimy, grey creature shot out of the hole.

It had sharp teeth and black holes for eyes.

Smelly green snot was dripping out of its nose.

Nadia and Amy screamed and ran out of the room.

Chapter 3

Trapped

Nadia and Amy came to a door, but it was locked.

The scratching was getting louder and louder.

Lots of the slimy, grey creatures were crawling down the walls towards them.

"Help!" yelled Nadia, banging on the door.

"Someone wake up and help us!" shouted Amy. "These things are going to attack!"

The slimy creatures were getting closer.

Their sharp teeth were snapping at the girls' feet.

Green snot dripped down the wall.

The smell made the girls feel sick.

"What have you been doing?" shouted a voice.

It was the Manager.

"Help us!" shouted Amy. "We are being attacked!"

"I will help you this time," said the Manager. "But why did you upset my Wall Crawlers? They are my little pets."

"Come with me, little ones,"
said the Manager.

And the smelly creatures went with her
back to their hole in the wall.

Nadia and Amy went back to their rooms, but they knew that they would not get any sleep that night.

Questions
Chapter 1
Where does Nadia think the noise is coming from? *(page 6)*

Why is Nadia scared? *(page 11)*

Chapter 2
What does Nadia think might be making the noise? *(page 14)*

What do the Wall Crawlers look like? *(page 18)*

Chapter 3
Why did the girls feel sick? *(page 24)*

What does the Manager call the Wall Crawlers? *(page 28)*

About the Author

Tim Collins has written over 90 books for adults and children.

He enjoys reading horror books and playing computer games.

He's stayed in lots of scary hotels, but none of them were haunted as far as he knows.

About the Illustrator

James Lawrence loves reading comic books.

He lives in Manchester and he spends his days drawing cool pictures.

He thinks he could survive a night at the Horror Hotel.